09/01/1998

Olof and Lena Landström

WILL GETS
A HAIRCUT

Translated by Elisabeth Dyssegaard

R&S
BOOKS

Stockholm   New York   London   Adelaide   Toronto

Rabén & Sjögren Stockholm

Originally published in Sweden by Rabén & Sjögren
under the title *Nisse hos frisören,* pictures and text copyright © 1991
by Olof and Lena Landström
Library of Congress catalog card number: 93-660
Printed in Denmark
First edition, 1993
Second printing, 1994

ISBN 91 29 62075 9

Will is going to get a haircut.

Mama says Will should look nice for the end-of-the-year
school party.

Then she goes shopping.

Will has to wait his turn.
He looks through some magazines. The pictures are boring.

No, one picture is nice!

Now it's Will's turn.

"Like this!" says Will.

"Hmm," says the barber.

Then he begins to cut.

He cuts and combs and cuts…

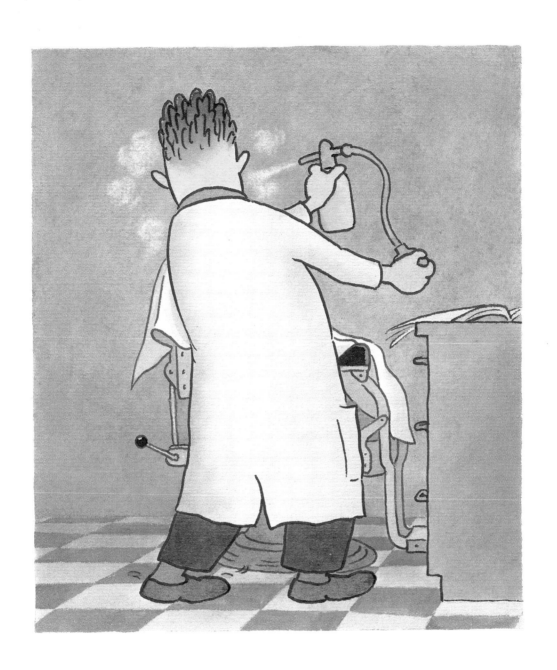

and combs and cuts and sprays.

Now Will is done.
It's exactly what he wanted.

"My goodness," says Mama.

Will is pleased.

But now they have to hurry to the school party.

It will begin very soon.

Mama and Will run the last bit of the way.

They make it just in time.

Everyone is already there.
"Is that Will?" says the teacher.

"How neat," whispers Susan.

When they finish singing, the teacher talks for a while.
Then everyone says goodbye.

Afterwards Will has to explain how the barber did it.

On the way home, Mama offers a special treat.
Will wants an ice cream.

He chooses strawberry.
Mama gets one, too.